André
THE FAMOUS HARBOR SEAL

By Fran Hodgkins
Illustrated by Yetti Frenkel

Dust-jacket and interior design by Chilton Creative

Printed in China

O.G. Printing Productions, Ltd.
Kowloon, Hong Kong
March 2011

6

ISBN 978-0-89272-594-6

Library of Congress Control Number: 2003107967

BOOKS·MAGAZINE·ONLINE
www.downeast.com
Distributed by National Book Network

DEDICATION

To Winston and Rosie, for everything
—F. H.

To my parents, for their love and support
—Y. F.

*H*arry Goodridge was a man who loved animals—any animal and every animal, whether it walked or flew or swam. But Harry especially loved one animal, a seal called André.

André was a seal who loved people. He loved grown-ups, and he loved children who played on the beach. But he especially loved one person, a man called Harry Goodridge.

This is their story, and it's all true.

One spring day, Harry borrowed a friend's boat and went searching the harbor of Rockport, Maine. He knew these waters well; he was the town's harbormaster. But on this day, Harry wasn't working; he was looking for a seal pup to keep as a pet.

At that time, it wasn't against the law to catch wild seals and other marine mammals. Today, nobody is allowed to even touch one unless he or she has a special permit. But in 1961, there was no law against what Harry planned to do. He had raised two other seal pups, but they had not lived to become adults.

This time, Harry was determined that things would be different.

Soon he and his friend spied a pup bobbing in the waves, with only its big, round eyes and the top of its head in sight. The men drew near, and the little seal looked up. Then he swam right over to the boat, as if it were an island ferry he had been waiting for.

9

10

Harry took the seal pup home to meet the family—his wife, his children, and their many pets. The Goodridge children shared their father's interest in animals. At times the house had been home to dogs, cats, rabbits, chickens, a pet robin, and—of course—the two harbor seal pups just like this one. The family named him André.

At first, André spent his days in the yard and his nights in a bathtub in the basement. Twice a day, Harry took him to Rockport Harbor for a swim.

Once André learned to eat fish, his routine changed. He spent the whole day, every day, in the ocean. Sometimes he would disappear overnight or even for a few days. During these times, Harry worried. Still, he told himself that if the little seal didn't come back, that was okay—he expected André to return to the wild someday. But almost every evening, André met Harry at the town float for a fish dinner and a ride home.

"Harry's little seal" soon became a familiar sight around the harbor. He would swim up to fishermen in their rowboats and let them rub his belly with an oar. He would nap wherever he wanted—in an empty dinghy, on a pile of rope, or on a lobster trap.

Harry knew that harbor seals are smart, so he decided to teach André a few tricks. The growing seal pup soon learned that if he rolled over, shook hands, or clapped his flippers, he would get a fish. At first, André would do the tricks just for the food. Before long, though, he was doing the tricks just for the fun.

People came to watch Harry and André at feeding time. The young seal loved their applause and laughter. Soon, dinnertime always meant a show.

ut Maine summers are short. Winter soon came, and Rockport Harbor became covered with ice. The only clear spot was André's entrance hole, where he met Harry for fish.

One morning, Harry woke up to a powerful winter storm.
He went to the harbor. The ice had broken up. Large chunks
ground against each other in the waves. André's hole was gone.
There was no way to know whether the young seal was all right.
All Harry could do was wait.

The weeks crawled by. In February, he got a letter that included an article clipped from a newspaper in Marblehead, Massachusetts, a coastal town about a hundred and eighty miles to the south. The article told about a seal named Josephine that had delighted local people with tricks. As he read, Harry became more and more certain that "Josephine" was really André. So, he called a relative who lived near Marblehead and asked him to take a look. But by the time the relative got there, "Josephine" had left.

Weeks passed. Then Harry got a phone call. André was in Rockland, just a few miles away—and he needed help.

Harry rushed to his friend's aid. It looked as if André had fought with another seal. He was cut and bruised, and one flipper was badly chewed. Many of his wounds were infected.

*T*o find out what to do for André, Harry called some experts. They told him that the seal would eventually die from his injuries. Yet Harry wasn't going to give up. He called the veterinarian who took care of the rest of the Goodridge animals. Dr. Mac gave André some strong antibiotics. The medicine worked, and the seal recovered.

The next summer, Harry and André made up some new tricks. All of them grew out of things Harry had seen the seal do as part of his natural behavior. For example, when André stretched, he would sometimes cover his eyes with a flipper. He quickly learned to do that when Harry asked, "Aren't you ashamed of yourself, André?"

Sometimes, when Harry had a particular trick in mind, the seal had to figure out what he was being asked to do. So, he would try several different tricks. When he did the right one, Harry's praise and a fish for a reward let André know he was correct. And once he learned a trick, he never forgot it.

21

The harbor seal's fame spread beyond Rockport, beyond Maine, even beyond New England. Newspapers and magazines from all over the country told the story of André and Harry. Visitors came to Rockport especially to see the harbormaster and his animal friend.

When summer ended, Harry again had to figure out what to do with André. He couldn't leave him in his summer pen because the ice that always formed in the harbor would crush it. So, Harry moved André into a friend's boathouse.

Miserable, the seal spent his time gazing out the window at the sea. Harry visited him regularly, but André remained glum. One day, a big storm blew in, so Harry brought the seal home and put him in the basement. In the morning, André was gone. Harry discovered a pile of snow on the floor. The seal had pushed out a window and slithered over the snow to the water.

Harry called the newspapers to alert people that André was loose. Soon, he got a phone call from a town fifty miles away. He drove there and brought André home again.

Late the following fall, Harry decided to let André take his chances in the wild. After all, the seal wasn't a baby anymore, and others of his kind managed just fine in the ocean over the winter. The experiment succeeded, and Harry and André developed a yearly routine. The seal spent the winter at sea, then in the spring he returned to Rockport and his pen.

Even though André was full-grown, Harry worried about him during their months of separation. The seal still faced possible harm in the stormy Atlantic. Maybe what André needed was a winter home where he would be happy.

Harry found him one—about two hundred miles to the south, at the New England Aquarium in Boston. Several other harbor seals lived there, so André would have their company, be well fed, and—most of all—be safe from the dangers of the winter ocean.

The aquarium was happy to have such a famous guest. That fall, aquarium workers picked up André in Rockport and took him to Boston by truck. When word spread that this special seal was at the aquarium, crowds of people came to see him, just as they did in Maine.

New England
Aquarium

25

When spring came, the aquarium called to ask Harry when they should bring André back to Rockport. "Don't," Harry said. "Let him swim home." But Boston Harbor was full of large ships, like freighters and oil tankers. Everyone worried that André would be injured if he were let go at Long Wharf. Instead, the aquarium decided to truck André to Marblehead and release him there.

Harry met André and the aquarium people in Marblehead on the day of the release. They loaded the seal onto a boat and chugged out into Marblehead Harbor. Once they reached open water, Harry said, "Go home, André!" The seal leaped off the boat and vanished into the water.

Would he find his way back to Maine? Did he want to? After a winter in captivity, would he decide to spend the summer at sea instead of in his cage in Rockport Harbor?

As Harry drove home, he wondered.

WELCOME HOME ANDRE !

A few days later, the phone rang. A fisherman had found André curled up in his dinghy, sound asleep. Soon, another call came and then another, all from people who had seen the seal. Each sighting was closer to home. Then there was one last call—from Rockport Harbor. André was home!

For eight of the next ten years, Harry's harbor seal spent summers in Maine and winters either in Boston or at the Mystic Aquarium in Connecticut. His fame continued to spread. The Rockport town manager named André the town's honorary harbormaster. And in 1978, André helped unveil a life-size statue of himself. Made of polished granite, it looks out to sea even today.

Andre at age 18

28

In 1985, Harry learned that his old friend was nearly blind. The lenses in André's eyes had become so cloudy that he could no longer see. Despite the loss of his sight, André managed just fine with his other senses—especially smell. Everyone agreed that he could swim home.

And so he did, traveling from Cape Cod to Rockport—nearly 300 miles—despite being blind. Asked how André did it, Harry could only tell the newspapers, "I've asked him, and he won't tell me."

Although André could no longer see well enough to do some of his tricks, the shows went on that summer. When winter came, the seal made his usual trip to the aquarium in Mystic. But this time, he didn't settle in. Instead, he refused to eat no matter what he was offered. After nearly two weeks, Harry decided it was time to bring André home. He drove to Mystic and picked up his old friend. When he got home to Rockport, André ate.

In 1986, André turned twenty-five, and that spring—as usual—he set out to find a new mate. Normally, the competition to win a mate energized him. Not so this year. On June 14, André was seen in Rockland looking tired and bruised. He had probably lost another battle with a younger, stronger male seal. He avoided all humans—even Harry.

A month later, Harry found his old friend. André had died on a deserted beach in Rockland. Harry took the harbor seal home and buried him.

Four years later, Harry Goodridge died, too. But, no one in Rockport—or Boston or Mystic—will ever forget the remarkable friendship between the man who loved animals, especially one seal, and the seal who loved people, especially one man.

GLOSSARY

Antibiotic: A kind of medicine that helps the body fight infections.

Boathouse: A building that boats are stored in to protect them from the weather.

Captivity: A place where a person or animal can't roam free.

Dinghy: A small boat, usually a rowboat, that is used to travel from a dock to a boat tied up in the harbor and back again.

Floe: A large piece of ice.

Harbormaster: A person in charge of a harbor.

Lobster trap: A rectangular box made of wire mesh, baited with dead fish, and then set on the bottom of a harbor or bay to attract and catch lobsters.

Mammal: A kind of animal that has hair, is warm-blooded, and feeds its babies milk.

Routine: A regular, set way of doing things.

Veterinarian: An animal doctor.